MAY TURPIN,

THE

QUEEN OF THE ROAD.

A ROMANCE.

By the Author of " Dick Turpin, a Romance of the Road ;" Jack Sheppard and Jonathan Wild,' &c., &c.

RICHLY ILLUSTRATED.

THE NEWSAGENTS' PUBLISHING COMPANY (LIMITED), 147, FLEET STREET, E.C.

1864.

MAY TURPIN,

THE

QUEEN OF THE ROAD.

PROLOGUE.

THESE chronicles of the interesting career of one whose life has hitherto been zealously kept in the dark records known only to a few, will doubtless now cause some surprise to a large class of readers with whom the name of Dick Turpin is as familiar as "Household Words." Why the Biographers of the renowned highwayman have never introduced the name and daring deeds of Turpin's protegee and worthy successor, the dashing and danger loving May, has long been a wonder to those who have been fortunate enough to trace the important reports which were left by her to tell the story of an eventful life.

Such reports will form the groundwork of this romance, and the reader will find every page of this exciting history fully prove the trite proverb that "Fact is stranger than Fiction."

The quiet old city of York seems closely associated with the name of "Dauntless Dick" and his "Bonny Black Bess."

Coming from Dringhouses, along "the Mount," towards Micklegate Bar, as the pedestrian strolls leisurely from Knavesmire towards the ancient city, the first object which will arrest his attention and win his admiration is the square tower of the grand old Minster.

Massive and magnificent does that ancestral pile appear rearing its head cloudward.

Passing on through the Bar and walking down Micklegate to Ouse Bridge, as you look towards Fulford, memory recalls the scene of the fatal fall of "BLACK BESS" after her wonderful ride from London to York.

A feeling of sympathy for poor Turpin, robbed of his beloved steed and constant companion, naturally pervades the mind, until we almost regret that justice was so close behind the hero of the road.

York Castle still holds the "gyves" which Turpin wore, and supplies the curiosity seeker with other relics of the celebrated Dick, that "skilful surveyor of highways and hedges." One of the most important of those relics are the private papers upon which we found the new romance of MAY TURPIN.

BOOK I.

CHAPTER I.

A HEROINE.

"Such a face,
It made the sunshine of a shady place."
DRYDEN.

Crack, crack, went the whip of a dashing young lady mounted on a lovely, but spirited horse, and at the sweet sound of the fair rider's voice, forward sprang the noble animal. On and on, without one halt, clearing hedges and ditches, high and low. For six miles, without one pause she kept her measured pace towards the City of York, as the Minster clock struck with solemn sound the hour of seven, the tone reverberating on the morning air.

"Halt, my lady!" said a voice, as suddenly the form of a gentleman sprang from behind a hedge and quickly laid his hand on the neck of the beautiful horse, who started back, and then remained passive as a lamb.

"Release him, sir" said the rider, patting the neck of the affrighted animal.

"Nay, my sweet rider," was the courteous reply, spoken in the mildest and most winning tones.

"Who are you?" asked the lady with perfect self-possession.

"My name is a terror, and I would not willingly frighten you," replied the intruder, " but, if you wish it, I will tell it you, upon one condition."

"What is that?" she asked.

"That you will first tell me your own," replied he.

The tones in which he spoke, were so soft and melodious, his manners so gentle and yet impressive, that they could not possibly have caused any feeling like fear to enter the thoughts of his lovely companion.

She looked at him with a stern and scrutinising gaze, but the light of her eyes changed in an instant to a soft and pensive expression of intense admiration.

"My name, sir, is May Melville, and my father's house is but one mile across the fields, to the left of Rawcliffe."

"May Melville," muttered the cavalier, tapping the ground with the end of a small whip. He placed one arm across the neck of the horse, with his face towards his new acquaintance, and looked up into her face with an intensity of expression, that rivetted her gaze for a moment, and suddenly the crimson flush that stole over her features, as her lovely eyelids gently fell, told him too plainly that a spell of love sudden but deep was stealing as surely into her heart as it had into his own.

"Come, sir," said May Melville, trying to hide her confusion, "You remember your promise. Yonder comes one of my father's servants to find me, and I must leave you. Come, tell me quickly, sir."

"What is your name?"

A sudden spasm shot through her, as she remembered his last answer, that his name was a "terror."

She gathered the reins in her hand and prepared to start off, on the instant.

"Good morning, sir, will you kindly let me pass? I am expected home."

"Certainly, my charmer, I wish I might go with you," answered the mysterious stranger, as he stept back for the horse to start.

"Good morning, my dear Miss May," said he, with a smile, "we shall meet again, and soon."

"Never!" was the instant reply, "Never, unless you tell me and at once, who you are!"

He paused for one instant, with his eyes fixed upon hers, as she darted away, with an expression of disappointment clouding her fair face.

A voice sweet as music followed her, though the words fell like a death knell on her ear, as her companion behind said, my name is

"DICK TURPIN."

She turned to give one look at him, a look of wonder, melting into admiration, and as he kissed his hand to her, the horse gave one bound over a hedge, and hid from Dick's view, Miss May Melville.

CHAPTER II.

THE SECRET GATHERING.

"Each one in his time plays many parts."—SHAKESPEARE.

Literature has a mission, pure and ennobling. The philosopher and poet should be the missionaries of truth, and purity. No less holy an office has the romancist. Fiction should be the eloquent advocate of her solemn and august sister Truth, winning by silvery sounds an audience for the stern teachings of her less fascinating but invaluable companion. Sad, indeed, is the influence of that debasing and disgusting libel upon literature which now teems from an over prolific press. More sad still is the state of mind which those vile, contaminating, and over wrought "sensation stories" superinduce upon the minds of the infatuated readers. Pandering to the vilent passions, succumbing to the very lowest instincts, and vitiating every idea or sense of refined taste, week by week the English press (that boasted glory of this Christian country!) sends forth a tide of impure and debasing "literature," a disgrace to the authors and a curse to every reader.

Every romance should have an aim. But what can we say of these false fictions, either the matter or the ability? Do they

> "Point a moral, or adorn a tale?"

No!

It can scarcely be a matter of wonder that thousands of educated men, and women too, denounce, without reserve, all works of fiction. Thus the historic lore and masterly style of Walter Scott, the wonderful photographs of real life as depicted by the miraculous pen of Charles Dickens—that magic master of pathos and humour—are to them works almost unknown because they are "fictions." And for the same silly reason are they kept from the glorious wealth treasured in the writings of England's greatest novelist—Sir Edward Bulwer Lytton—novels, which, for classical learning, purity of sentiment, profundity of thought, beauty of language, and elegance of style, are unsurpassed by any writer in any known tongue. The names also of Thackeray, Currer Bell, Anthony Trollope, and a host of other giant intellects of the present century, who have laboured hard to make the vocation of a novelist noble and honourable, will ever stand as denouncers of the petty and soulless imitators, who, for a paltry pittance, prostitute both time and talent. This class of literature is both contemptible and mischievous. We find in these productions filth and immorality, without the voluptuous gorgeousness which distinguishes the *amours* of a sensuous lady of high rank, from the low debauch of a gin drinking, disgusting female costermonger. In both cases the word impurity is, perhaps, as just, but beyond all question that which is condemned by society as utterly opposed to all principles of right and wrong, in the one case, is in the other received, acknowledged, and even applauded. It is to this latter description of depravity that we now allude.

The reason we have made the foregoing remarks is, that we shall be compelled in the course of our history to depict scenes of low life, and introduce disreputable characters.

We are anxious while doing so, that they should not cause a blush to stain any sensitive cheek, and we will paint the scenes delicately and in the mildest colours that the truth of the narrative will permit, trying to "please all, and offend none."

* * * * * * * * *

Within sound of the bells of St. Giles's Church, there stood a miserable dilapidated house, on a spot now known as Great St. Andrew Street. The door was open night and day; a long passage with two steps midway, led into a large back yard, closely surrounded by crumbling walls and tottering sheds.

A stranger upon going into this yard would have felt convinced that it was empty, but a frequenter would go straight across to a door facing the passage, and knocking loudly three times, would speak in a whisper a mysterious word, and enter.

It is a cold, windy night, following the day before Christmas eve. Wild gusts of fierce wind rush lawlessly from east to west, cutting the poor traveller through to the bones as he keeps on his way towards the secret gathering place.

Hurrying on, he scarcely meets a companion in that wintry walk.

He turns sharply into the passage, pushing the door back with a bang, and feeling his way cautiously up the two steps, crawls along straight to the private door; he gives three decided raps, and waits nearly a minute before he receives an answer.

At length the door opens.

A voice asked the pass word.

"*Ninnyne,*" replies the traveller.

The door flies open, and he walks boldly into the room.

"What, ho! my mummer," cries a dozen voices; "welcome, once more among the mummers." "You are a stranger."

"I am," was the laconic reply; but I have much to tell you.

CHAPTER III.

"THE MUMMERS."

"All the world's a stage."—SHAKESPEARE.

The "mummers" were a body of the lowest thieves and cracksmen of the day.

The club consisted of about twenty sworn members, and among them were some of the most celebrated highwaymen whose very names were words of terror to a traveller. The room in which they nightly met was a spacious wooden one, large enough to hold three times their number. It was very roughly but strongly built, and disgustingly dirty. If "cleanliness is next to godliness," then that place was suited to be the home of vice. A large table ran the length of the room, and seated round it our traveller found more than a dozen men. Drinking and singing were the principal objects of attention when he entered, but scarcely had he uttered the words "I have much to tell you," 'ere a general move took place, and a seat at the head of the table was made vacant for him, while nearly every voice shouted "Three cheers for the king of the mummers," and the unanimous yell that shook the air on that bitter, cold December night, left no doubt of the loyalty of the "king's" subjects.

He was a fine handsome man.

Tufts of jet black hair fell gracefully over a noble forehead as he removed his hat, and with a quiet "Thank you, my lads," seated himself on his temporary throne.

"Hot brandy, boiling hot, and quickly, too" said the king of the mummers to the landlord of the "mummery"—for such was the sign of the house where this vicious crew met.

The brandy was placed before the chairman, who seemed deeply wrapt in thought. And as he sat there with his eyes vacantly fixed upon the upper end of the room, his thoughts evidently wandering far away, let us describe him.

He was a man of about five feet eight inches in height. His figure slim, but well built, with a broad and manly chest. A good head was well balanced upon a pair of expansive shoulders; and there was a reckless carriage about him, which would at once attract attention. The first feature to excite the admiration of a beholder was the eye. Clear, cold, and thrilling was the look from those dark eyes as they let their full gaze fall upon any person. It was a look before which few could keep control over their features or feelings. Long practice had taught the owner of those beautiful orbs to make good use of them, and many a time to them, as we shall hereafter relate, Tim Clipton, the king of the mummers, owed a favor, and often a lucky escape. His mouth was firmly set, with just a slight sense of humour playfully haunting the corners, which made him appear even younger than he really was. His age was twenty-two. He was at times lively and witty, but often reserved and thoughtful; still he always had full command of his temper, and, and while there was a determination in his utterance, and a firmness in his manner which threatened danger to any foe, there was ever a kindness in his tone and an urbanity towards one and all, which made him a great favourite among every circle into which his chequered career led him.

Such was Tim Clipton as he sat there, in a deep reverie, while his companions impatiently awaited the recital of his story.

Suddenly Tim started, and clapping his hands with a forced assumption of joviality, cried out "Give us another song; come, its a bitter night, and Christmas time, let us be jolly."

"A song, a song," reiterated several voices.

"Come, Young Shakespeare, you give us a song," said Clipton to a thin and hungry looking man, who sat near the other end of the table. He was called "Young Shakespeare," because he had been a strolling player previous to joining the ignoble "mummers."

"With all my heart," replied the lean youth, laughing as an overture.

"Stow your clatter," demanded the king, and silence reigned over the meeting for a moment, when "Young Shakespeare," in a boisterous and most unmusical voice, bawled out the following ditty :—

"ALL THE WORLD'S A STAGE."

Old Shakespeare, told us long ago,
From infancy to age,
That all mankind were players,
And "that all the worlds' a stage."
  Chorus.—And that all the world's a stage.

A bad wife plays the devil on earth,
And storms and rants and teases,
But a sweet tempered wife will play
Which part her husband pleases,
   So all the world, &c.

Some people will in earnest play,
While others play in jest,
There's many play a double part,
But fair play's always best,
   For all the world, &c

The wife will sometimes play the truant,
The husband play the scrub,
The scrub will play the gentleman,
And the gentleman the scrub,
   So all the world, &c.

Oh! my, how folks mistake their part,
By taking that for this,
The little miss will play mamma,
And fat mamma play miss.
   I'snt this world a stage ?

The prude will play the hyppocrite,
The wanton the coquette,
Old maids will play the solo part,
Brisk widows a duet.
   To prove the world's a stage.

The fribble plays the monkey's part,
While full of roars and revel,
We "mummers" are such jolly dogs,
We play the very devil.
   All the world's, &c.

But when these trifling scenes are past,
And life's last act is over,
Then death will let the curtain drop,
And we shall play no more.
   So all the world, &c

Who played cobbler,
Who played king?
Will not be then the jest;
The only question then will be,
Who played his part the best?
   Oh! this world's is a stage.
   Oh! this world's is a stage.

"Bravo! bravo!" shouted and encored every one in the room.

"Now, Captain Clipton," said "Young Shakespeare" musing, we must hear your story.

"Yes, yes," again urged the company eagerly.

"You shall, said Tim," while a frown gathered upon his brow and a melancholy expression clouded his features, as he placed his right hand into his breast pocket, and withdrew a glittering jewel, placed it upon the table.

It was at once the object of interest to every member of this club of criminals.

Instinctively they glared and gloated upon it.

At that instant a tramp of feet was heard along the passage as of persons coming nearer and nearer to the room.

Quick as thought every one was on the alert.

The landlord rushed to the door, and listening intently gave a low whistle, only to be heard in the room.

In less than one minute the glasses of liquor were seized, three trap doors in the flooring were opened, and all save, Tim Clipton, had descended into the cellars.

Tim dashed out the lamp, and as two officers walked into the room, the king of the "mummers" quietly laid himself upon the floor in one corner of the room and feigned sleep.

CHAPTER IV.

THE HAUNTED GRANGE.

"Can such things be, and overcome us like a summer
Cloud without our special wonder."—SHAKESPEARE.

Scarcely three miles on the north road from the now thriving town of Liverpool, in the year 1710, there stood a huge mansion. It was surrounded by very extensive ground, long walks, and bordered on the east and south aspects by a large copse.

A very old but stately building was "Fallowfield Grange." It had long been untenanted, for it had twice been the scene of such domestic affliction as to render it an unpleasant habitation for its owners. They had not only left it, but totally neglected its fastly decaying walls, until ruin seemed to claim it as its own, and devastation held undisputed sway over the whole property.

Rumour had long whispered that the place was haunted.

Such was the legend through Lancashire, and the traveller when passing would scarcely deign to give a momentary glance at the mouldering mansion. It is nearly the end of December; the north wind is coursing in its mad career over wild and wold.

The clouds have all been swept from the face of the heavens, and the clear, bright moon pours down a flood of silver light upon the crisp and frost-covered ground. The road is clear, save one figure, which steals silently along the side of a hedge, watching its own shadow creeping closely behind. It is the form of a man, wrapped from head to heel in a long loose cloak. His arms are folded; and he seems so perfectly alone and at ease, that he whistles a favorite tune as he strolls on towards "Fallowfield Grange."

Turning at three cross roads he halts, for he is a stranger to the place. Scanning the old Grange at a glance, he again strikes off in a path to the right, and once more falls into his listless and moody manner of walking.

With ears as keen as the biting wind which chilled his very blood, he suddenly detected a sound as of an object gasping near him. He listened intently, scarcely breathing for a few seconds. He distinctly measured the heaving breath of some large animal which seemed to be suffering pain. "What can it be," he muttered. "I must and will find out."

He commenced his search, and about fifteen yards from where he first stood, discovered a beautiful colt, lying on the cold ground, behind a cluster of close furze. He walked up to it, and kneeling down patted the lovely creature on the neck.

It was evidently not a wild one, as the condition of its coat and general appearance showed him clearly that it was well cared for, and probably, that was the reason it suffered so much, being now unsheltered during such a cold and bitter night.

The traveller rose, and taking off his large cloak, hung it upon the furze while he divested himself of an under garment, which he gently placed upon the shivering animal, and gathering a quantity of furze and loose leaves, he covered it well over, and for a time left it.

Throwing his spacious cloak on again, and pulling it tightly around him, he turned towards the Grange, but had scarcely moved when his attention was arrested by the sound of horses' feet along the high road, which he had just left. He hid himself to listen, but placed himself so that he could see any object moving along the highway.

The moonlight revealed to him two men, mounted.

They were evidently farmers, and in close conversation.

"We must capture him before we return," said one, in a loud burly voice.

"I will never go back until I do." was the reply, spoken in a milder and more impressive manner by his companion.

They started with wonder as they heard their own words repeated by an echo in the distance.

The air was so keen and the silence so impressive, that their words were reitterated as distinctly as though some one had mocked them at their elbow.

The secreted cavalier tried to move towards the spot from which the echo proceeded, but found his cloak caught so often in the hedge, that with one bound he came straight out into the pathway, and walked towards the high road.

"Who goes there?" said he, snappishly pretending that he was startled at the appearance of the intruders.

"Who are you?" was the expected reply.

"I am the new owner of Fallowfield Grange."

"Indeed, oh! indeed," were the ejaculations of the now bewildered countrymen.

"I wish you good night gentlemen" said the new owner.

"May we know your name, sir, and are you a stranger to these parts?" asked one.

"No! I'm no stranger" said he, "and my name is—DICK TURPIN!!"

CHAPTER V.

LOVE'S DAWN.

"Parting is such sweet sorrow,
That I could say good night until to-morrow."
SHAKESPEARE.

Seven long days had passed since May Melville had leapt over the hedge and disappeared from the admiring gaze of the notorious highwayman. Seven weary nights had gone tardily by, during which the lovely May had dreamed incessantly of the manly form and courteous bearing of the fascinating stranger, who in one moment had caused a revolution in the thoughts and opinions which eighteen years had formed in her pliant mind. Day by day had she thought of that winning face; night by night had she again in blissful dreams heard the sweet accents of that melodious voice, the tones of which held her as a charmed and willing listener. May wondered where she could have heard that name before, for certainly she had heard it. From north to south, and east to west of England the name of Dick Turpin had flown like a winged omen scattering seeds of fear in a thousand breasts. "Dick Turpin" was a synonym of terror, and at the very name hearts beat quicker, and cheeks were blanched.

Cautiously did May utter the name to friends, inquiring who and what Dick Turpin was, but the blank expressions and wondering looks which were her only answers, added mystery to mystery. She at length determined to learn all, cost what it might.

Seven days had passed and May was straying down "the King's Walk," on the banks of the Ouse, when she saw there was but one person to keep her company along the esplanade. It may be a matter of surprise to our readers that Miss May Melville should be allowed to walk alone on a public esplanade after dark.

We will, therefore, at once introduce to the reader's notice the home of the fair lady and the position she occupied therein.

May had lost her mother when she was ten years of age. Her father was a stern and methodical man, who had, from some imaginary cause, disliked his only child from her birth.

She therefore had grown up to the age of ten, petted and spoiled by her mother, chided and shunned by her father.

Soon after she was sent to school at a large establishment in Lancashire, called "Fallowfield Grange," which for years had held a reputation unsurpassed in the north of England. She returned to her home a self-willed, petulant and imperious young tyrant. She would stand gazing into her father's eyes with a determined look of rebellion, and a scornful curl upon her lip, until he quailed before her daring gaze, and with a sad sigh, hurried away to hide his impotent rage.

May Melville, from her figure and carriage, would be called a fine girl, with a bold, almost impudent look, there was a devilry in her manner, and an abandon in her general deportment which foretold no moral supremacy in her character. Her face was round and full, with a nose well proportioned, and thoroughly characteristic, her mouth was prettily shaped, while her eyes would have led many a willing slave to desperation, perhaps to worse,—death.

For miles round her father's farm, May was known as a wilful and daring young lady, whom no one could equal for horsemanship.

She could dash across field, or leap a hedge with any lady known in old Ebor.

Her name was as well known within the sound of the cathedral bells as the tones which hourly chimed from the famous tower.

Still her company was not sought by her own sex. There was a masculine tone about her character, which constantly kept her fair friends, from too close an intimacy, but if ever there was a lady friendly on the instant with gentlemen, it was May Melville.

She walked gently along "the King's Walk," with her eyes fixed slyly upon the one close by her side.

She was pleased because it was that of a gentleman, and as the closely muffled figure strolled along, scarcely a yard from her; while passing underneath one of the lamps that hung from the old walls, May started at discovering that her companion was

"DICK TURPIN."

She made a sudden halt, afraid to pass on, and turned towards the edge of the river counting the beautiful pale stars, which were reflected in its placid bosom.

Turpin heard the sudden stoppage of the tiny feet on the gravel walk, and seemingly indifferent, but anxious for any episode to enliven his monotonous walk, he carelessly turned towards a rough wooden seat, fixed for weary travellers, and throwing himself upon it, began to follow his favourite occupation, whistling a tune fit for any meeting of the "mummers."

May waited several moments, then walked gently on, carefully keeping close to the river's edge, but as she drew near to the seat, whereon Turpin rested, she trembled visibly, and for once lost her self possession.

The wary Richard noticed the stranger's embarrassment, and looking from under his eyelids, at once recognised his fair lady of the early morning ride.

Not the slightest indication escaped the cautious highwayman. Still he whistled; still he gazed on the stars with an absorbed and wondering stare, until the trembling May summoned courage to pass on.

A sound arrested her progress as instantaneously as though a thunderbolt had fallen in her path.

It was the voice of her dream, saying "my dear Miss Melville, you must be lonely. Do you spurn me so cruelly?" May started and approaching him, sat down by his side.

CHAPTER VI.
LOVE'S SUNRISE.

"There is nothing half so sweet in life
As love's young dream,"—MOORE.

The meeting of the two lovers, for such they unquestionably were, was at first formal and cold.

Turpin knew woman's character too well to entrust the secret of his passion to May too soon.

May had just sufficient vanity to "assume a virtue if she had not," and kept a reserved but dignified air, with consummate skill.

By nature May was a perfect actress.

With good sound sense and quick perception, she had a comprehension of all points of a character at a glance.

No less remarkable also, was her intuitive identification of thought and feeling with any character which occupied her attention.

It was her habit to assume new manners and develope fresh characteristics in every circle of acquaintances into which she was introduced.

Much deeper was her anxiety, and far more careful her tactics, if that circle included gentlemen.

Such circles only were sought out by her, and if any cause was wanting to make her more distasteful to her own sex, it was found in the fact that May Melville was so clever an actress, that few gentlemen could withstand her fascinating manners and winning ways.

As she sat on the seat by the river's side, a lamp shone directly upon her face, making her features distinct and clear to Turpin's gaze. His face was in the shade. She felt his piercing eyes were fixed upon her, and gradually the icy tone of her voice changed. Her manner became less reserved. She spoke with a frankness that had a greater charm for her watchful companion, than all the artificial tones or looks which she could so easily command.

"Will you tell me where you live?" asked Turpin with his eyes looking into hers, to watch the effect of such an inquiry upon her mind.

"Oh! yes," she replied. "My father keeps Clifton Farm, nearly an hour's walk from here, on the road to Stockton." She paused an instant, then with a deep sigh, added in a feigned tone of dejection, "I wish I was going away from him."

Her eyes were slowly lifted up to read the impression of the last sentence upon the listener.

Turpin's look was steady and searching, he changed not a muscle of his features. Not a shade of light in his eye told her the rapid thoughts and fancies which her sighing wish had given birth to.

"Why would you leave him, my dear Miss May?" asked the highwayman in a quiet, measured manner.

He had an object in the inquiry and eagerly awaited the reply.

"Because my father hates me," was May's quick and emphatic answer.

That answer settled a thousand doubts and fears in Turpin's brain.

That answer at once determined him in his course of action.

As he sat gazing into the face of his fascinating companion, reading her character by every look and word, an idea had flashed across his mind with the rapidity of lightning.

And as the lightning often leaves behind, its fiery credentials of ruin, so had that one thought set on fire the brain of the reckless robber.

"Will you go with me?" was the question Dick at last mustered courage to ask.

He leaned forward to catch the answer, but quick as thought he recovered his self possession, and threw himself back against the arm of the old seat, as though the question was no more than a pleasant piece of fun, and not intended to demand a reply.

May did not answer it, but a light shot from her eyes, and her cheeks turned deadly pale.

She turned her head to hide her emotions, or to get time to master them.

Not one movement escaped her companion.

"Come," said he, "it is growing late. You have a long walk before you. I will go with you towards Clifton Farm."

The stars were shining brilliantly; the soft, tender light of the pure moon fell like a veil of silver over the face of nature. All things breathed peace and serenity as the two lovers strolled back along the road towards May Melville's home.

To all outward appearances the two companions were as silent and cold as was the lovely night on which they took that walk, which so altered their future lives and bound their fates together.

Not a sound passed the lips of either. The only sounds they heard were the measured echoes of their footsteps on the crisp earth, relieved by the booming of the Minster clock, as its sonorous notes told forth the chimes, and the lingering sound seemed to float on the air until they faintly died away in the distance.

All without was calm. But within the breasts of those two silent pedestrians what a world of tumult was raging.

Passion and reason were at stern war. In May's bosom there was a fierce revelry of lawless fancies. Glowing dreams haunted her imagination. Pictures too beautiful and thrilling to dwell upon were conjured up by her uncurbed imagination, which had ran mad.

Visions of a reckless but happy life, with the stranger who now walked so closely by her side, new life, new scenes, new hopes and aspirations, new acquaintances, and new admirers. For a time she was almost delerious with the crowding thoughts which rushed through her brain.

Turpin's mind was deeply perplexed.

His dearest project on that night was to get May to leave her father's, and join him in his famous exploits of crime.

It was a matter of difficulty even to his prolific invention, to form plans suitable to his ulterior purpose. He knew the character he was dealing with, and prudence was very necessary. The power Turpin held over her, increased now nearly to infatuation, was his principal reliance.

Not for a thousand May Melville's would the clever and wary highwayman yield up the independence of his character. It was his greatest charm in private life, and his guardian genius in every public enterprise.

He was not over anxious to draw an immediate answer to his important question as to whether May would go with him.

Time might assist him he thought, and he was yet desirous of testing the temper and spirit of his fair friend.

On and on they walked, slowly and mutely, until within a few yards of Clifton Farm.

"I will wish you good night," now said the highwayman, "we may be seen, and you would not like that, I am sure."

"Why should you think so?" asked the cunning young lady, with a sly peep at the face of her companion.

"When may I again meet you?" was his evasive reply.

"To morrow evening, at nine o'clock, in the Minster Yard," she answered.

"In three days I shall leave York for London, and probably shall not see you more than once again, Miss Melville."

Closely he watched her features, as he deliberately modulated each sentence, with marked emphasis, and in his most winning tones.

May's hand had been gently taken by him, to bid her good night, and he felt a tremour run through her frame, as he spoke the last words.

"Only once more," she said, as if talking to herself.

"Unless," said Turpin, pausing, "unless you will answer my question."

"What question, sir?" inquired the artful coquette, in an arch and innocent tone.

"I will give you until to-morrow evening to decide whether you will leave Clifton Farm, and go with me to London. Good night. At nine o'clock in the Minster Yard. I will await you."

"Good night, sir" was all May replied, but the language of her eyes told plainly that "Yes" was resting on her sweet lips, and she longed to utter it, but prudence sealed the ruby casket, and the important mony-syllable died upon her tongue.

She turned away towards her now more wretched home, while he who claimed every thought of her mind and wish of her heart, started briskly off to the city in the distance.

CHAPTER VII.

THE CLUB OF CRIMINALS.

"Justice is a halting Beldame.—SHAKESPEARE

The officers of justice who had entered the "mummery" demanded a light of the landlord, and were surprised to find the rendezvous so empty at that hour, on such a cold night.

They well knew that, unless plunder, or perhaps, murder, called the "mummers" away, there was sure to be a number of them assembled at their chapel, as they called the "mummery."

It was the first time these officers had ever been enabled to get an entrance. They knew the pass word, and thus obtained admittance without obstruction.

The landlord was dumb foundered.

On opening the door to listen, he did not recognize the footsteps, and consequently gave a low thieves' whistle, which meant danger.

The password being so readily given, he was thrown off his guard.

He procured a light for the officers, and seemed quite bewildered as he asked them, who or what they wanted.

They did not condescend to answer, but snatching the light, they caught a glimpse of Tim Clipton's prostrate form on the floor, in a distant corner of the room.

They made their way across, and holding the light over the "king of the mummers," whom they believed to be asleep, they held a consultation.

"That's him I think," said the elder officer, a strong rough fellow.

"I wonder if he's got the article on him? That will soon settle it," rejoined his assistant.

"You hold the light while I search him;" but be on the alert, he's a very desperate fellow. Take this," said he, giving him the light, "and if he's got it on him, I'll find it, or my name is not Waters."

"Will you my pippin, not if I know it," muttered Tim to himself.

"You keep clear Nabbit, in case he resists, stand by his feet, and shade the light from his face with your hand.

Nabbit went to the feet of the prostrate "king," but scarcely had raised his hand to shield the rays of light from the features of Tim Clipton, 'ere the highwayman, with a dexterous spring, knocked the light up into the air, and throwing himself upon the floor, seized Waters by the legs, fairly lifting him off his feet, and threw him with a heavy thud to the other side of the room.

THE WITCH'S WARNING.

The officers were paralysed.

The movements of the notorious Tim were so unexpected, and so expertly managed, that his opponents were powerless.

Tim gave three rapid stamps upon the floor.

And before Waters could regain his feet, or Nabbit recover the useless lantern, the three trap doors flew open, and up came everyone of the "mummers" with a shout of triumph enough to shake the old building to the earth.

Nabbit and Waters made for the door.

But they were surrounded in an instant, and after a desperate struggle pinned to the wall.

The din of oaths, orders, and ejaculations, were perfectly bewildering.

"What shall we do with them?" asked those who held the officers in their iron grips

"Tim, what's to be done?"

The king had been silent from the moment the trap doors had opened.

He knew his men could master twenty officers at any time.

"Bind them and take them down into the "Devil's Den," shouted Tim, then let every man return to this room quickly, I want you all.

The officers were bound and locked in the "Devil's Den," the strongest cell underneath the mummery.

Another light had been brought in by the landlord.

"Come lads, fasten the trap doors, and listen to me," cried Tim.

They all clustered round in a circle, as their king, pale as death, took a pistol from his side pocket, and quietly cocking it, began to address them.

"Am I your king?"

"Yes, yes," was the unanimous answer.

"Have I the right to be so?" demanded he.

"Yes, yes," again answered his crew, with looks of surprise upon every face.

"Then I will act as such, 'honour among thieves,' lads, is our motto.   I have lost a most valuable jewel, since I came into the gathering to night, you all saw it, did you not ?"

"We did," was the general reply.

"Well, I want it, I must have it," said he, walking to the door, and deliberately placing his back to it.

"Not one man goes through this door alive, until I hold the "Ruby Heart" in this hand, *on my oath.*"

CHAPTER VIII.

THE NEW LORD OF FALLOWFIELD.

"Danger haunts that ruined Hall,
Dark and cold stretches the path
Unto its portals ; the great gods forbid
That thou should'st follow in it."—TALFOURD.

Turpin had visited "Fallowfield" but once prior to the night on which he met the two farmers on horse-back.

He knew all the torturous paths, and intricate walks, round the mansion, for his visit had been prolonged to nearly a month.   During that period he had never wandered outside the hedges which skirted "Fallowfield."

The farmers were so bewildered at the name of the new owner of the Haunted Grange, that they looked at each other in speechless amazement.

When they recovered their wits and tongues, they held a consultation as to what should be done.

Meantime Turpin had again commenced his favourite whistling amusement, and gone straight down the path leading to the back of the mansion.

He pulled from his belt a bunch of heavy keys, and had just coaxed the rusty bolt to yield, when he heard the subdued tones of the farmers becoming more audible as they followed him at a distance.

Dick flung open the heavy gate, carefully withdrawing the keys, and secreting himself behind a huge tree, awaited the arrival of his prying pursuers.

It was such a lonely spot, that Dick was panting for some amusement. If ever mortal man loved to challenge fate, Dick was that man.

Danger was his delight!

He would follow up an exploit simply because it was fraught with obstacles.

He would pick quarrels with desperate men for the more satisfaction of an hour's excitement, running into the very midst of destruction for the pleasure of escaping.

Dick called it "Dodging Death."

The farmers still kept their seats as they neared the gateway.   They started with affright as they heard a pistol report, and a shot went whizzing right over their heads.

They were both armed, but with only one pistol each.

They cautiously entered the grounds, and cast a glance round to discover their enemy.

The brilliant light of the moon made the trees stand out in bold relief, while every object was seen as clearly as at noon-day.

Dick's shadow as thrown on the snow, at last caught their eyes, and they demanded of him to come from behind the tree.

Quick as an echo the dauntless Dick stept out in front of them at about twenty yards distance.

"What do you want here?" asked Dick in a very imperious but assumed tone.

"Your head" shouted both simultaneously.

"I am obliged to you for your kind feeling," said Dick with his well known musical laugh, "but I think its possible I shall require it myself to-night."

"Then we'll take your life at once if you resist us; take care, and come while you have a chance, Dick ?"

"Ha! Ha!" rang loud and clear on the midnight air, and echo answered "Ha! Ha!" a score times over hill and dale.

The farmers began to show signs of temper.

That was Turpin's cue, he longed for that, it meant danger.

He came about three yards nearer to them, and looking calmly at them, snapped his fingers loudly before them.

"There, gentlemen, that is the value I set upon your wants or wishes.   You may value my head, but on my word, as a gentleman, you shall not take it with my permission, and I doubt the probability of your doing so without."

This was said with such deliberate insolence, yet with so much ironical politeness, that it exasperated one of the burly countrymen.

Ere his companion could stop him, he aimed his pistol at the impudent highwayman and fired.

Turpin detected the movement just in time to pop behind the tree as the ball went crash through the bark, and pierced a hole through Dick's cloak.

"Thank you for the attempt," said the fortunate tantaliser as he again walked into the path and stood as a target for the remaining pistol of his antagonist.

"Yield, or on my oath I will shoot you like a dog," shouted the owner of the loaded weapon.

"Shoot my buck, shoot, I rather like it," answered Richard laughing again at the farmer's impotent rage.

Scarcely had the words escaped his tripping tongue before bang went the pistol, away whistled the shot, while the excited countrymen dashed their horses forward to look at the corpse of the prostrate Turpin.

"We had better get assistance without delay," suggested one, and off they galloped back through the gateway, towards the village.

As they passed the end of the path, to reach the highroad, they were startled at the voice of the undying Dick, who once more sent his melodious "Ha, ha" of derision after them, but this time he accompanied it with a bullet.

Dick never shed blood from mere wantoness and cruelty.

He fired to frighten the retreating fools, who had amused him for a time, and at last been the dupe of such a simple ruse.

When the last pistol was fired, Dick fell forward on the snow, nor moved again until he heard the deceived countrymen turn their horses' heads to "get assistance."

At these words Turpin was compelled to put his cloak over his mouth to stifle his laughter.

He rose and hurrying down the lane, managed to arrive in time to see them pass within two yards of him, and he fired the harmless shot, to get rid of them more rapidly.

Turpin now pulled out his keys again, and was just entering a door leading into the mansion, when a crash was heard from the inside, and a voice inquired,

"Who's there ?"

Dick stood surprised, as he only had the keys which admitted to Fallowfield Grange.

Who could be within?

CHAPTER IX.

THE WITCH'S WARNING.

"A wicked hag, and envy's self excelling
In mischief, for herself she only vext."—SPENSER.

The booming sound of the clock striking the hour of nine rolled over the city of York, and died away silently in the distance, as a horseman well wrapped up, rode sharply up through Bootham Bar, to the gloomy gates of the Minster.

It was Dick Turpin!

He threw himself from his horse, and, tying it to the railings, walked boldly up the yard on the Stonegate side.

Three times he paced backwards and forwards, casting impatient glances at the entrance, while his ears were on the alert for the slightest sound. He at length came back to his horse, and leaning his arm across its neck, awaited the arrival of Miss May Melville.

At last she came, flushed with excitement, and trembling with fear lest the idol of her heart should have doubted her word, and refused to wait.

Turpin's manner was at first formal and reserved.

"Well, Miss May," said he, taking her hands in his own, and looking full into her face, "what is your answer? Will you go with me?"

Turpin had determined that if May had declined, he would treat her with the profoundest respect, and start from York to London that very night.

"Yes, I will, and to-night," was May's immediate answer, spoken with such emphatic earnestness that Dick was convinced of its truth by the very tone of the utterance.

Turpin threw open his arms, and the next moment May Melville and the notorious highwayman were locked in such a passionate embrace as only true lovers can feel or describe.

Turpin had arrived at that period of life when a man feels a wonderful change in the current of his feelings.

The impassioned enthusiast, and the man of reckless daring, are at all times the most keenly susceptible to love.

When that passion once assumes the sceptre, there is no check upon its emotions and no escape from its excitement.

Turpin for the moment was proud of his conquest, as he felt the warm breath of his lovely companion close to his cheek.

May did not attempt to release herself from her blissful imprisonment.

She was willing to be locked in those arms for hours.

She reclined her head on Dick's shoulder, and for a few seconds their breaths came shorter and quicker with the sudden thrill of joy. Turpin drew her closely to him by placing his arm around her waist, and, for the first time, imprinted upon her willing lips a fervid kiss.

A thrill of inexpressible pleasure ran through the blood of the yielding girl, such rapture was to her as novel as it was welcome, and for a few moments, all thoughts of home, father and friends, were banished, while she gave heart and soul to the maddening feelings and delerious sensations which stole over her as she felt the arm of her beloved one pressing her to his bosom.

The appearance of a figure coming towards them in the distance, awoke Turpin from his dream of delight. He released May and untying his horse, lifted his fair companion on to it, then vaulting into his seat behind her, he gave her the ends of a long sash, which he had put round his own waist, and told her to fasten it tightly around her own.

The stranger, as he reached them, saw a fiery horse, rear itself with a double burden, and at a word from its male rider, bound forward and start away with the speed of the wind.

On they sped through the sweet night, over fields, through valleys, up hills, and over hedges they flew without one interruption, trees flashed past them, old tottering villages, were no sooner seen looming before, than they were left behind.

On, and on they dashed, in spite of the cold north wind, which came rushing over the open country, into their very teeth, almost stopping their breath.

The silence was broken by Dick, as he patted his treasured horse on the neck.

"Bravo! '*Devil May Care*,' bravo, you will carry us far on our road, yet before the sun gets up."

The lady clung closely to her lover, she was bitterly cold, but cared not for that, it was her first taste of the new life before her, the excitement kept her hopes high and thoughts elate.

Turpin's brain was busy plotting and planning the future career of his trusting companion.

He had marked out in his own mind, a brilliant career for the one who was that night so tenaciously clinging to him during that mad ride, through those weary miles.

A village clock was timidly proclaiming the hour of ONE as though afraid to break the death like silence which slept over the scene, when "Devil May Care" dashed past on her wild career, neighing and snorting, steaming with the effects of struggling up the village and sniffing the fresh breeze as it met his dilated nostrils.

The village seemed to fly back as the equestrians rushed on into the open country once more. They galloped off furiously down a hill, which so terrified May, that she flung her arms around her leader's neck, and begged him to stop.

Dick was deaf to all entreaty, he knew the distance they must go before they reached any shelter. He was, also, half mad with the excitement of his race against time.

He had gained a rich prize!

He loved and was loved. His world of joy and hope was clinging round his neck with all the energy of a passionately loving and trusting woman.

What more could he need to make his brain intoxicated? He felt her warm breath on his cheek, and her head pillowed on his heaving breast. He was mad with joy.

The night was serene and inspiring, the air keen and cheering, while the north wind braced his nerves and made him feel like a giant.

Still he sat on his horse as light as a feather, and in his exultation cheered the noble creature on to meet repose with the break of the coming day.

The horse on reaching a short curve of the road suddenly started as if shot. Some living object was heard moving behind the hedge. Dick drew in the reins, and leaned forward to discern the cause, as he loudly demanded in a very angry tone that the intruder should stand out.

A wild shriek rang out from the hedge, and scarcely had it ceased before the name of "May Melville," pronounced in an unearthly tone and solemn manner, reached the ears of the affrighted riders.

May trembled violently. Fear is contagious, Turpin could not shake off a feeling of dread.

It chained him to his seat!

Had Dick been alone on that horse, he would have leapt off in an instant, and dared death.

But the sweet charmer of his new love was holding him in fetters he could not break. At the sound of her name a thousand phantom fears crowded before him. Terror paralysed him. The dreaded thought that might lose her rushed upon his mind, and he grew desperate.

"Stand forth, whether man or devil!" shouted Turpin.

The object did stand forth, but it was neither man nor devil.

It was a female form—a witch!

Lean, haggard, ill-looking, and badly clothed, there stood the figure in the pale moonlight. She looked like a shadow!

"Filthy hag, who are you, and what do you want?" asked the infuriated highwayman.

"That Lady, I want, May Melville, she knows me— Miss May knows Grace Howell well."

Dick turned to learn the truth of the witch's words.

"Yes, she's a witch long known in York," said May.

"My mother knew her long before she went mad, they call her the "Old Owl.""

"Yes, yes, I'm "Old Owl" now, they mock me now, but I will save her. Yes, I will save Miss May Melville, then I can die."

"She is going to London with me" said Turpin, "so stand aside!"

"No, Dick Turpin, I know you, I hate you."

"Will you let me take my young lady back to Clifton Farm?"

"No, curse you, no" answered Dick.

"Ha! ha! Richard Turpin, curse away, it hurts not me, but I will curse you for years to come. I will track you all through your life, I will foil you at every turn, until I rob you of May Melville, or see her dead at my feet."

"Look there, Dick Turpin, look there," shrieked the hag, as she whirled round and pointed to a distant hill.

On the summit of that hill, in terrible relief, covered in a silver shower of glittering moon beams, hung a horrible spectacle.

It was a gibbet, ghastly but grand was that scene.

The excited and impatient lovers on the affrighted horse, the old exulting witch, with her bony fingers pointing to that hideous object on the hill.

The figure swaying to and fro in the cold night wind, and the brilliant beams of the lovely moon, playing about the pallid corpse as if in mockery.

Turpin's eyes followed the direction in which the cursing and shrieking phantom pointed.

There was an awfully impressive silence for a few moments.

The "Old Owl" broke it with another yell, as she strode up to the horse, and seizing the reins, made the horse plunge and start forward.

Dick put his spurs in, and away they flew over the prostrate form of the screaming witch. Still her wild words followed them.

"I will see you swinging there yet, Dick Turpin, curse you! Mark me, I will."

These were the last words heard.

The distance deprived Turpin or May from hearing any more of the fearful curses of the "OLD OWL."

CHAPTER X.

THE "DEVIL'S DEN."

"Abandon hope all ye who enter here."—DANTE.

The "mummers" were thunderstruck at the extraordinary conduct and tone of their king.

"Search everybody!" was the general cry.

"Yes, yes; search us!" again repeated many of the principal members of the club.

"I will," answered Tim, who was getting more deeply incensed at the slight chance of recovering the missing jewel.

In the excitement and confusion, one remarkable looking man stepped forward, while his comrades almost held their breath at his defiant bearing towards the dreaded Clipton.

"What jewel is it that you have lost?" asked the man.

"What is it like, and the value of it?"

"Priceless, Spitfire," replied Tim.

Spitfire stared as his king continued—

"It is a ruby heart, set round with diamonds, and I will sooner lose my right hand than part with that gem, it belongs—well, never mind—I will have it, or look out, lads!"

There was a flash in the dark eyes of the criminal leader which threatened danger.

Spitfire was a man of desperate energy and most daring courage.

He was one of the first and worst members of this band of remorseless marauders. His word was as much respected as Tim's, but he had not the appearance nor the noble bearing of the kingly robber. Nature had stamped the villain on every feature of his repulsive face.

As Spitfire saw the angry flash from the eyes of Clipton, he well knew that a storm was brooding, and little as he cared for himself, yet he feared the lawless monarch of the "mummers" might inflict summary chastisement upon some helpless and unoffending member.

"Will you be searched by me?" shouted Spitfire.

"Yes," cried one and all.

He commenced his unwilling task, but failed.

Not a sign of the "ruby heart," was detected.

Tim Clipton stood silently against the door, his arms folded, his brow knit, and one finger upon the trigger of his too fatal weapon, woe be the wretch upon whom the treasure was found, seemed to be the language of those burning eyes, as they were fixed upon each member as Spitfire pursued his fruitless search.

"Are you satisfied now?" asked the relieved searcher, turning with triumph towards the king.

"No" said he, to the evident astonishment of all.

"Where is Will Filcher?" quietly but emphatically asked Clipton.

The fact that Filcher was missing flashed on one and all immediately.

The landlord was summoned and interrogated as to whether any footsteps had passed through the passage since the officers entered.

He thought he heard some one slip from behind the door, as the candle was dashed out when the alarm was given.

Clipton cursed Filcher loud and long.

"Clear the chapel, shouted he," all of you except Spitfire, and meet me here to morrow night at ten.

Out into the cutting night air trundled the miserable thieves one by one. Silently they skulked off, muttering between their chattering teeth oaths of discontent.

Tim Clipton fastened the door, and bidding Spitfire descend with him, they went down to the "Devil's Den."

This place of concealment was a wretched vault underneath the road. It was cold, damp and cheerless. A trembling lamp hung from the ceiling, shedding a ghastly light upon the one table and three chairs that furnished the den.

Two long forms ran along each side close to the wall.

Tim and Spitfire sat down on two chairs. They called for bottles of brandy, and commenced smoking.

Waters and his assistant stood pinned to the wall, with their mouths gagged.

Clipton for a moment forgot his loss, and burst out into a merry laugh at the helplessness of his prisoners.

Their faces wore a most revengeful look.

The kingly "mummer" placed his chair at a respectful distance, and amused himself by aiming corks into the gaping mouths of the irritated officers.

Spitfire begged that the gags might be removed; he was not a man to cause unnecessary pain.

Although his face was so repulsive, nature, as usual, had redeemed herself by giving him a compassionate heart.

The gags were removed. A groan at the other end of the cell, startled the boisterous robbers, as they were singing snatches of vile songs, recording dark deeds, to annoy the myrmidons of justice.

Spitfire turned full round.

A human being was struggling to rise from the ground, but he incessantly fell back as fastly as he rose.

The next instant Spitfire was across the room, and throwing the figure upon its back, for the faint glimmer of the lamp to fall upon its face, he cried out, " its Filcher."

Clipton leapt from his chair at the sound. He shook Filcher so violently that the intoxicated wretch soon became aware of his position.

"Where is it," roared Tim, seizing the half-awakened man by the throat.

"Where is what?" stammered he.

"Give it to me, or die, you dog."

Another severe shake accompanied these words, which completely brought the quaking thief to his senses.

"What is it you want of me, Tim Clipton?" asked Filcher, in a steadier tone.

"The jewel."

"The what?"

"The jewel, you know; come, no tricks with me, or I'll strangle you on the spot."

"I have not got any jewel, noble captain."

"You lie; why did you come down here and hide? eh? give it to me at once, or I will serve you the same as I will those officials yonder, put a bullet through your brains."

He said this with such earnestness, that Filcher clearly saw he must adopt some ruse, to allow his infuriated master to cool down.

"I saw something glitter on the floor upstairs, as we left the room," said Filcher, "let us go and look," he suggested.

"Come, then, and find it or lose your life."

Spitfire sat gazing at them during the conversation.

He was convinced Filcher knew nothing about it.

Tim led the way up the ladder to prevent Filcher escaping.

Meantime Filcher whispered to Spitfire "what jewel is it, what is it like?"

"A ruby heart, set with diamonds," was the answer.

At these words a glance passed between the officers, fully understood by each other.

Clipton searched in vain, and as his passion was expended, began to think from the manner of Filcher that he was innocent.

Tim ordered him to go below to send Spitfire up, and remain there.

Soon after, the trap door was let down and the three prisoners heard it fastened above them, followed by the tramp of their persecutors as they left the "mummery,"

locking the door on the outside and going away from the house.

Filcher was puzzled.

He sat on the table and stared at his imprisoned companions.

They stared at him.

"What do they mean to do?" asked Nabbit of Filcher.

"As far as I know, they intend murdering all three of us," was the consoling answer.

"Can you not help us?" inquired Waters.

"I can't help myself."

"You know the place, Mr. Filcher, come, so try."

"Oh, yes, I know the place, better than anyone of them, there's a long dark passage through that grating, leading down into the river."

"Untie these ropes, there's a good fellow."

"What will you give me," quickly asked the avaricous wretch.

"Anything in the world that I can give you."

"Do you know where that 'ruby heart' is?" asked Filcher, his greedy eyes twinkling at the suggestion.

"Yes, I have it," said Waters.

"Then, give me that," cooly replied the wily mummer.

Waters hesitated for a moment.

He knew that Tim Clipton would be there next evening at ten.

He thought if he gave it to Filcher he could easily overpower him if he got his freedom and recover it again.

"How could we escape even then?" asked Waters, to give himself time to think.

Filcher walked across to a large grating, resembling a door. He touched a spring and pulled it open.

"Down here," said he.

"Down the steps, to the right, you can walk straight to the river, to the left you can go nearly to Hampstead Heath."

"Good," said Waters. "Capital, we shall slip them; yet."

"Here my friend, come, loosen this arm and I will give you this valuable treasure, but mark me! keep it for yourself, Tim Clipton must not have it."

"Will you promise that?"

"Oh yes!" said Filcher, unfastening the benumbed arm of the grateful thief-taker.

The officers were bound both hand and foot.

Their arms were well confined, and tied to large iron rings, while they were closely pinioned and attached to a huge log of wood on the ground.

Filcher was a little more clever than the officer.

"Give me the jewel now," said the artful miscreant, when he had released the arms of Waters.

"Oh take those cursed ropes off my legs, I can scarcely stand."

"Not just yet," replied Filcher, holding the rope he had taken off the prisoner's arms.

He cautiously retreated out of arms reach.

Waters tried to coax him near.

"Here is the gem then, said the officer, take it Filcher, and let us all escape."

"I'm fly, old boy," 'throw the little valuable over here will you, you values your liberty, I values my nob, throw it over.'

Parleying was only waste of time.

Tim or his companion might return, and then escape would be hopeless.

Waters reluctantly threw the "ruby heart," into Filcher's ready hand.

He danced with delight. He could not estimate its value, but it was worth more than he ever had in his life before that he was sure of.

"Now then, look at that afterwards," cried out the impatient Waters, "let me free."

Filcher went through a pantomine of placing his finger on his nose, as he quietly closed one eye, and winked with the other, saying "not to night my dear Mr. Waters, it's damp outside, and you might catch cold."

The officer saw at a glance, the trap into which he had fallen. He grew desperate with rage, and with one powerful effort, slipped the cords round his legs so as to be able to get one nearly out.

One more try, a severe struggle. He was nearly frantic with rage. He had the strength of a giant, and snap went the last rope. He leapt out from his fetters towards the mocking thief. At the same instant Filcher flew on to the table, and with one blow of his fist sent the lamp flying across the cell.

Waters was lost in the dark. He listened a second, then darted to the spot where Filcher was creeping on his hands and knees. The officer made one clutch and found he had hold of the fugitive's neckcloth.

Filcher gave a lurch forward, nearly upsetting Waters, who, trying to pull the thief back, found he had but Filcher's handkerchief in his hand, while the owner had escaped. Filcher laughed out as the officer went rolling on his back over one of the forms.

A shuffling movement was heard for a few seconds as Filcher went towards the iron grating.

Another laugh, and "Good night, my lovely babies," was shouted out by Filcher.

Bang went the door of the grating, and the officers were left helpless in the "Devil's Den."

CHAPTER XI.

THE MYSTERIOUS SHADOW.

"The earth hath bubbles
   As the water hath, and these are of them."—SHAKESPEARE.

Turpin finding that the door of "Fallowfield" was barred on the inside, retired to the back to gain an entrance.

A faint light glimmered in the spacious hall, revealing the dim outline of a female form flitting about. It disappeared for an instant, then reappeared at the window of the first storey.

A blow at the window from some heavy object sent the glass raining upon the head of the astonished highwayman.

Turpin drew out a pistol and watched for the figure again to appear. Once more it came in bold outline, revealed by the light of the moon.

Crash went a bullet through the glass!

Turpin held his breath in suspense, his heart beat fast and loud, as a wild shriek, followed by a demonical laugh, rang through the mansion.

Dick, growing determined, tried another door, and after many attempts, replaced the keys in his belt. He threw off his cloak, and light as a squirrel he mounted an extensive outhouse, one leap, and he was hanging on the branch of a fine old oak, facing the balcony.

The bats flitted round and round him so quickly that he had to change his position, and sprang up to the coping of an archway.

From this position he could see every object in the room.

He sat cold and rigid until he heard a movement in the large room facing him, then lying flat upon the edge of the buttress, he carefully scrutinised every action of the mysterious stranger.

The figure approached the window.

Dick lay like a piece of solid stonework.

His figure was in the shade.

As the object of interest could not detect him, it opened the window and stept out into the balcony.

It was shrouded in a cloak from head to heel.

Turpin recognised the cloak as his own.

By a daring feat, almost miraculous, he flung himself off the coping stone on to the edge of the balcony.

When he got to the window it was closed and barred.

"Who the devil are you?"

"Speak, or I will never leave the spot and know you live," said Dick.

"Who am I?"

"Don't you know me Dick Turpin," said the female as she flung off Dick's cloak.

"I am the 'Old Owl.'"

He started with amazement at the face of the witch.

How came she there? what could she want?

"Why are you here, wretch?" asked Turpin. "What is it you want with me or my property?"

"I want May Melville, and I will have her," replied the hag.

"Why did you come here?" eagerly asked Turpin, thinking his residence at Fallowfield was an inviolate secret.

"I came here to bar up this house and keep May Melville out. You thought to bring her to this house to-morrow. Ha! ha! I have foiled you this time," said the witch with a deliberate but impressive earnestness, that made Dick listen in spite of his unwillingness.

"Hang you for a perfect fiend," said Dick in return, grinding his teeth with rage.

He seized his pistol and aimed it at her, but before he had time to fire, the hag had discharged one at him.

Luckily, a large bat flying past at the instant received the bullet and saved Dick's life.

"You are a bad shot, my hag," said Turpin, recovering from his surprise.

"I'll be more sure next time Richard, and that time will come" replied the "Old Owl," taking up the cloak and throwing it around her, she gave one fierce curse between her clenched teeth, and went into the interior of the house.

She did not return to the room.

After a long ambush Turpin descended, and went away from "Fallowfield" down the high road towards the North, for a priceless treasure he had left behind.

That treasure was *May Melville.*

CHAPTER XII.

THE LOVER'S FLIGHT.

"O woman! how much from that which she should shun,
   Does the poor trifler draw what charms her most."
                          BULWER LYTTON'S MSS.

When "Devil May Care" flew from the curses of the prostrate hag, he darted like an arrow along the road, with his double burden of love and crime.

Away the puzzled couple dashed through the woody country.

Still the hideous gibbet hung dangling before Dick's vision.

May was deeply wrapt in thought. She closed her eyes, and yielded to the gloomy fancies which came crowding in legions upon her troubled mind.

Turpin gave a glance now and then at her fair

face, and kissed her soft brow. She made no movement, but seemed in a deep trance of thought.

Dick urged on his horse, and. the contagious excitement of the rapid race began to be felt by both the horse and his master.

The earth seemed to fly beneath their feet, and the fleecy clouds to float swiftly over their heads, houses and trees, fields and hills, the woods and streams, again danced swiftly by, as they coursed on. Village after village, came and went. All nature seemed in a whirl until Dick began to grow giddy with the impetus of his rapid movement.

"Devil May Care" snorted and steamed, but never halted once, for more than thirty miles.

It makes the blood tingle at the very recollection of that glorious ride.

No wonder Turpin was in a delerium, as he gave his soul up to the full enjoyment of that maddening chase

"Hark forward! my beauty," was his constant and cheering cry.

The words, and the sounds of the voice which uttered them, were like new life to the noble animal.

He threw up his head in recognition of the command, and showed as much signs of delight as his master.

Dick tried to whistle but failed, and gave way to singing as a relief to his exhilarated feelings.

They tore up a long, steep hill soon after quitting the confines of Yorkshire, and upon reaching the base on the opposite side, coursed along a small plot of smooth ground until they came to a sudden halt.

Turpin was surprised at the slackening speed of "Devil May Care."

Breaking off in his song, he pulled up in time to save the horse from falling with fright.

The moon burst from behind a cloud and discovered a wide stream running swiftly in front of them.

Turpin sat a moment in deliberation, then turning his horse's head galloped back to the brow of the hill.

He made a fresh start, with a "Hark forward!" and away went "Devil May Care," with a daring plunge over the stream, coming down on the opposite bank within one foot of the water's edge.

The weight of his two riders and the desperate distance he had leaped, brought the creature down upon his knees, throwing May forward on to the earth.

She had fallen asleep, and awoke with a scream of terror.

The sudden shock and pain from falling upon her shoulder had given her a severe startling.

Dick with his masterly skill in horsemanship, kept his seat firmly.

He bounded quickly off the horse as it rose and stood trembling. Dick gave him one pat on the neck as he went round to relieve his less fortunate companion.

Turpin lifted her carefully up, and found she was little hurt, though much frightened.

She soon was enabled to be reseated, and with one of her lover's arms around her, away they started another stage on their long journey.

Two hours after this episode they arrived within sight of an inn.

It was an old-fashioned hostelrie, quaint in appearance and built in a most eccentric style.

It stood away from the road-side in a hollow, and was surrounded by stables, coach houses, and a very long garden. It also had an outlet down a long avenue of trees leading to a steep hill.

Among the wood which covered this hill forming the background of the inn, a mazy path had been formed, known only to a few, and made for the purpose of aiding any "gentleman in trouble" to escape.

The house was called "The Old Bell," kept by a retired smuggler, called "Silly Sting."

Sting was supposed to be the possessor of a wife "The wife" was a diminutive female shrimp.

She was fond of laughing and gin.

She had a florid complexion. Dark, hair combed back off a small forehead, little eyes, with a very devil lurking in their depths, a rather large nose, pouting, irresolute mouth, and, with an assumption of importance, she had not the manners to attract, nor the accomplishments to command attention or admiration.

Having. given this sketchy outline of "Sting's" beauty, as she appeared in the flesh, it may be as well to give an idea of her moral character.

It was so small that one or two words will photograph it.

"Narry," was the name Sting always called her by.

She could tell a good round lie with an oily tongue and steady eye.

Full of stratagem, and cunningly inventive, she never had a compunction at descending to any mean or despicable resource which could serve her purpose for the moment.

If our characters are reported by our actions, then it is only necessary to relate that "Narry Sting's," chief occupation in life, was to hatch petty plots of deceit, and get helplessy drunk. She varied this envious existence by a repetition of one or two pet sayings, about ten or twelve times an hour, when she happened to be sober.

Such was Sting's worse half, who will have to play a very important part in this romance.

Turpin was delighted as he descried in the distance, the dim flickering of a small light in a window of the Old Bell.

That light was a sign which Dick well knew the meaning of.

He awoke May, who had fallen into a dreaming doze as soon as she recovered from the shock of her fall.

"Hark away! my dear 'Devil,' look at that light awaiting us."

With another grand struggle, in a few moments the untiring creature stood bathed in foam, at the door of the inn.

Turpin pulled out a small silver whistle, and gave a low trilling sound through it.

He dismounted, and gave three loud thumps at the door.

It was opened instantaneously by the owner, who, in a gruff grating voice, as if he spoke through four asthmas said,

"Welcome Mr. Turpin," we expected you here, and my Narry made up her mind to keep sober."

Sting put his hand over the light, as he peered out into the breaking daylight.

"What's that, Master Turpin; a corpse, eh?" gasped the landlord, staring at May Melville, sitting like a frozen statue on the horse.

"It's a lady," said Dick, lifting her down, and leading May into the house.

"Narry, Narry," shouted Sting, "here's a lady, make haste."

The female shrimp came crawling out with extended mouth and half closed eyes.

She stood shivering in the cold morning air, smitten with the figure and dress of Turpin's favourite.

"Wake up, my good lady," said Dick, in a petulant tone, "conduct this lady to a room."

"I will return here to take her away to-night, about midnight."

"Give her everything she requires, and on no account let her be seen by a living soul."

"This visit must be kept a secret, Sting, mark me!"

"Shall I put the horse in the stable, Sir?" inquired the gruff landlord, nodding assent to Dick's caution.

"Yes, for one hour. Let me have some wine, and a good breakfast, before I start."

The sun was throwing his golden beams athwart the blue sky, while the fresh morning air came with a sweet and grateful relish to the jaded highwayman, as he again started from the "Old Bell," on his way to Fallowfield Grange.

After a weary day's travelling, he arrived at the village of "Flowerdale," three miles from the Haunted Mansion, and partaking of refreshment at the "Leathern Bottel," he left his horse safe while he wandered about to watch the moon rise 'ere he paid that visit to "Fallowfield," where he met with such a strange welcome from the "Old Owl."

CHAPTER XIII.

THE INVISIBLE HAND.

"How can we struggle with the invisible, who launched the world itself into motion; and at whose pre-decree we hold the dark bonds of life and death?"—BULWER LYTTON.

Millie Melville was one of the lovel'est girls that ever made a father's eye light up with pride.

Like a soft sweet gleam of sunshine, that fairy face was seen ever beaming with joy and intelligence.

Goodness always gives an expression of beauty.

Millie was as good as she was beautiful. She was as much loved for her goodness as she was admired for her loveliness.

Her face was a picture on which an artist would love to gaze, and in it he would find a spell charming him, until he became fascinated.

The brow was rather high and square, the cheeks were rather rounded, terminating in well a shaped chin.

The mouth was well shaped but rather severe. The delicately chiselled lips were full of character.

Satire seemed an artificial habit with Miss Millie, but it lent a definite characteristic to the expression of her sweet mouth.

The lips were rather too much contracted when the young lady was on her guard, but in her natural moments, humour seemed more at home, playing about the corners of those cherry like lips, and her laugh was the sweetest music ever heard on earth.

Upon looking directly into the face of the household fairy of Melville Hall, one thing would startle the beholder, sometimes jarring the impression of the other features.

Her eyes were extraordinary, like her mouth, they were the medium of artificial expression. By nature they were large and lovely, guarded by the most luxuriant lashes that ever hid light and lustre from woman's most attractive charm—(save her *tongue!*)

The eyebrows were not arched, but nearly straight, or rather more like Hogarth's "line of beauty."

The *tout ensemble* was most charming, but for the constant theatrical expressions of the eyes.

There was a fire in them when excited like—what? —most like a tiger's, a fearful glare, it chilled the blood, a fiery frenzy seemed to smoulder in them and of a sudden light up and deal death to every object upon which their glare settled. But they could melt with pity and move the sternest heart.

Her hair hung down in long curls below her waist, a shower of rich and clustering ringlets.

Her figure was not *petite*, her height about the middle stature. She was moulded in one of nature's most perfect moulds, and proud indeed must nature have been of her lovely representative.

Her step was light as a snow flake, her carriage like a queen's, and most royally did she wield her sceptre, never fearing a lack of subjects over whom she could throw the spell of her "majestic" accomplishments.

Miss Millie Melville was deeply indebted to nature, but no less so to art.

Her intellect was almost masculine.

She was the very counterpart of her father, a man eminent for his mental powers and erudition. Her education for the period of which we are treating was a miracle, but no expense had been spared to render her the glory and hope of her loving parents.

Such was their constant desire, and such was the realisation of their ceaseless anxieties.

Melville Hall, was an old but magnificent mansion, off the high road from Knottingly to York.

It was ancient and capacious. Surrounded by old coach-houses, and very large grounds.

It was an isolated dwelling, high up on a steep hill, with an immense park running round, bordered by high hedges.

It commanded a very extensive view of the woody scenery of the county.

Melville Hall and its owners were better known all through Yorkshire and Lancashire than any families in the county.

They were as much respected as they were well known.

The mansion had been the habitation of the Melville's for more years than any living memory could record.

The present owner was Sir John Alexander Melville, whose family consisted of Lady Melville, Miss Millie (or more correctly Emily) Melville, and Miss Caroline Melville.

Sir John was an eccentric but worthy man, about forty-two years of age.

He would sit for hours deeply engrossed in study. Study was his pleasure.

Lady Melville was somewhat younger than her husband, but of an imposing and stately mien.

A well shaped face, long and full, with profuse and beautiful dark hair, a good eye, small mouth, motherly expression, and as good a heart as ever beat in human breast, were the attractions of the lady of Melville Hall.

Miss Caroline was nearly as much like her mother in character as her sister was like her father.

As gentle as a dove, with a sweet winning expression, angelically mild and pensive was that dear Caroline.

"A lovely creature, far too good,
For human nature's daily food."

Miss Millie was twenty, and Caroline eighteen years of age, at the time when the following circumstances occurred.

It was a lovely summer's evening, one of those glorious evenings when the blushing sunset floods the earth with a sea of health.

The sun was grandly drooping behind the Wolds in the distance, shedding sheets of refulgent light over the whole aspect at the back of Melville Hall.

The very heavens seemed on fire, and the slanting rays, as they fell on the sward, seemed to resemble bars of molten gold.

King "Phœbus's" chariot rolled along the sapphire-paved streets of the celestial empire.

The amber sea waved to and fro over the western horizon.